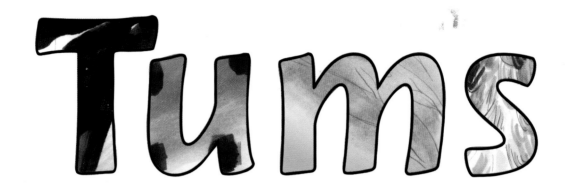

Tums

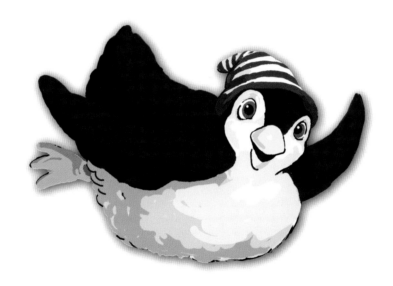

David Bedford and Leonie Worthington

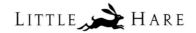

LITTLE HARE

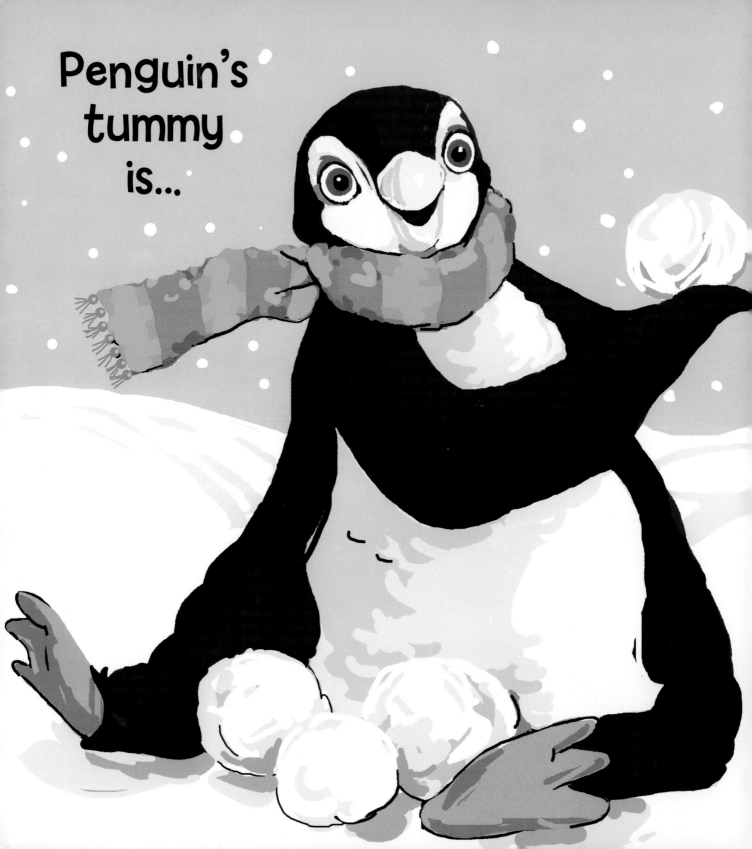

Penguin's
tummy
is...

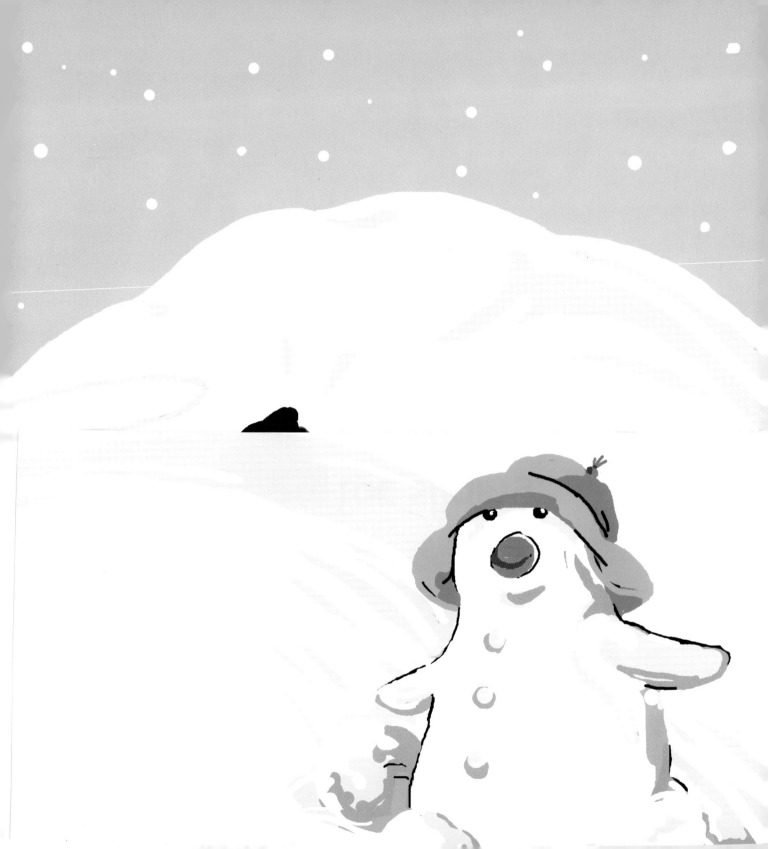

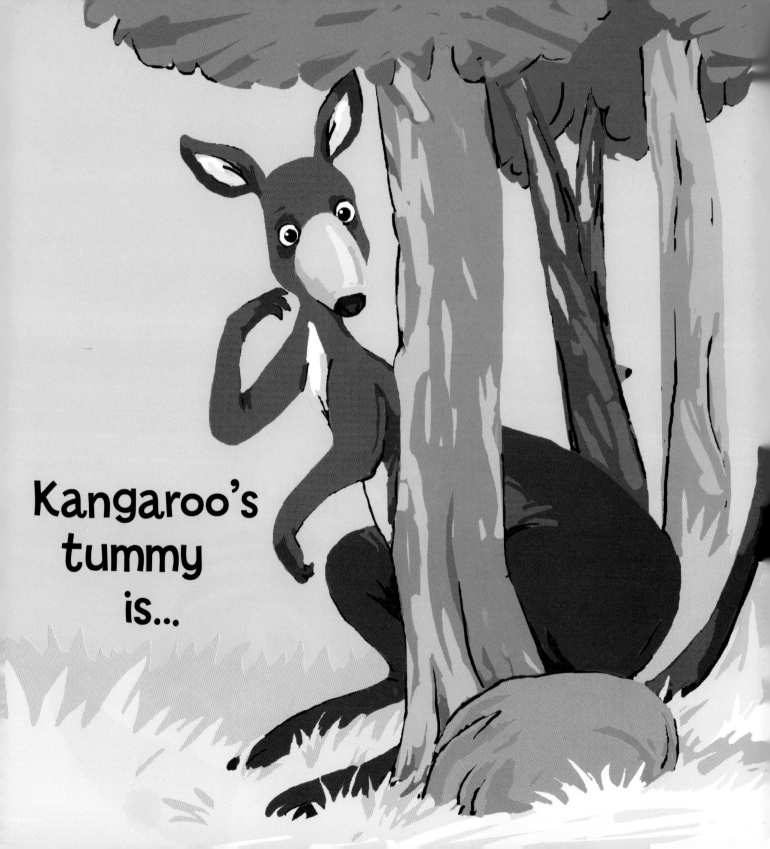

Kangaroo's tummy is...

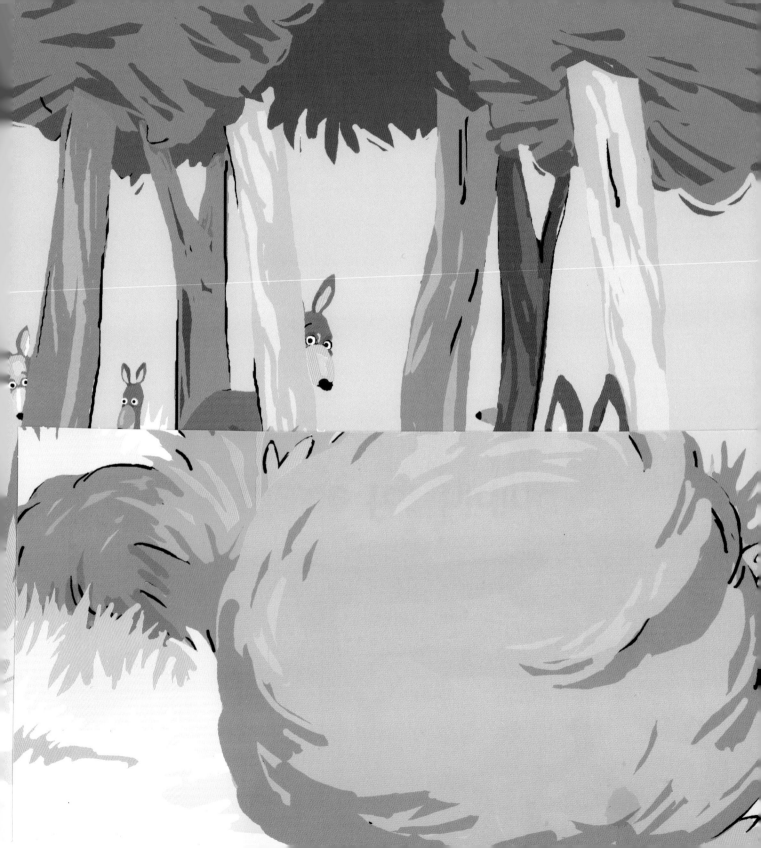

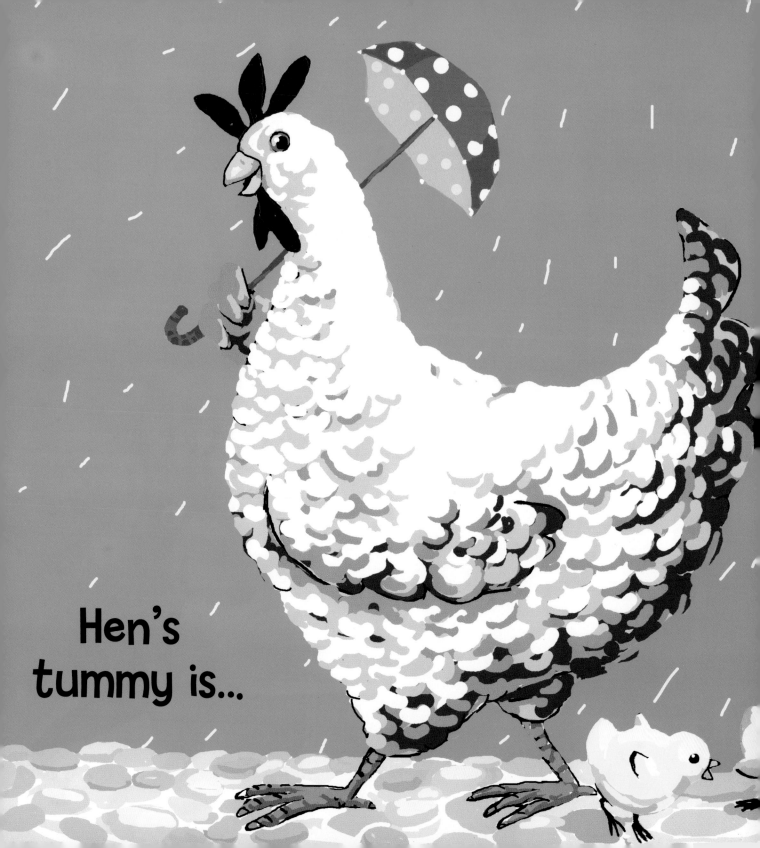

Hen's
tummy is...

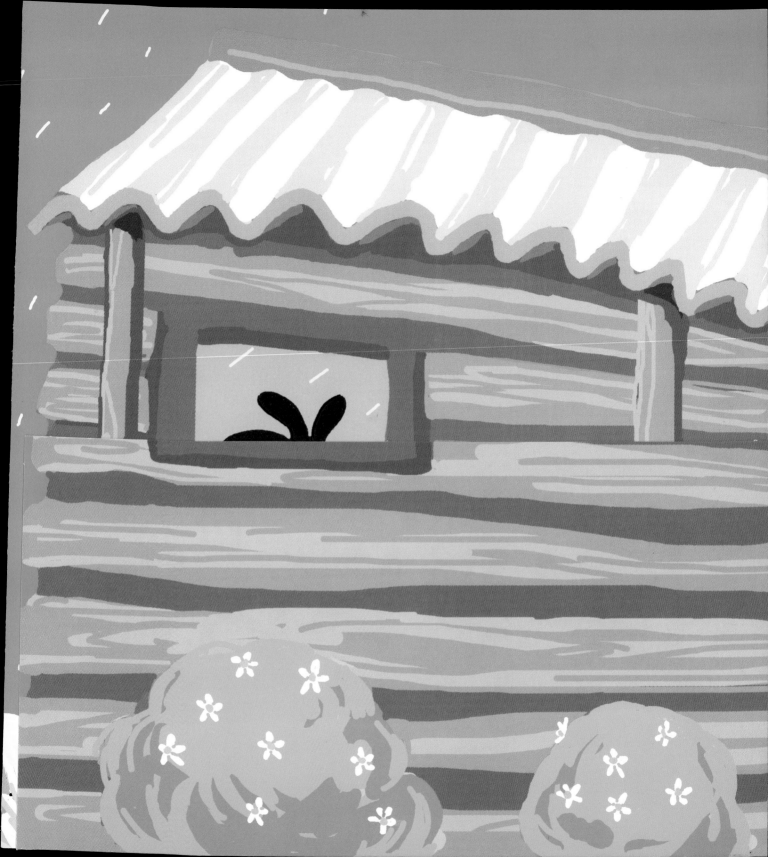

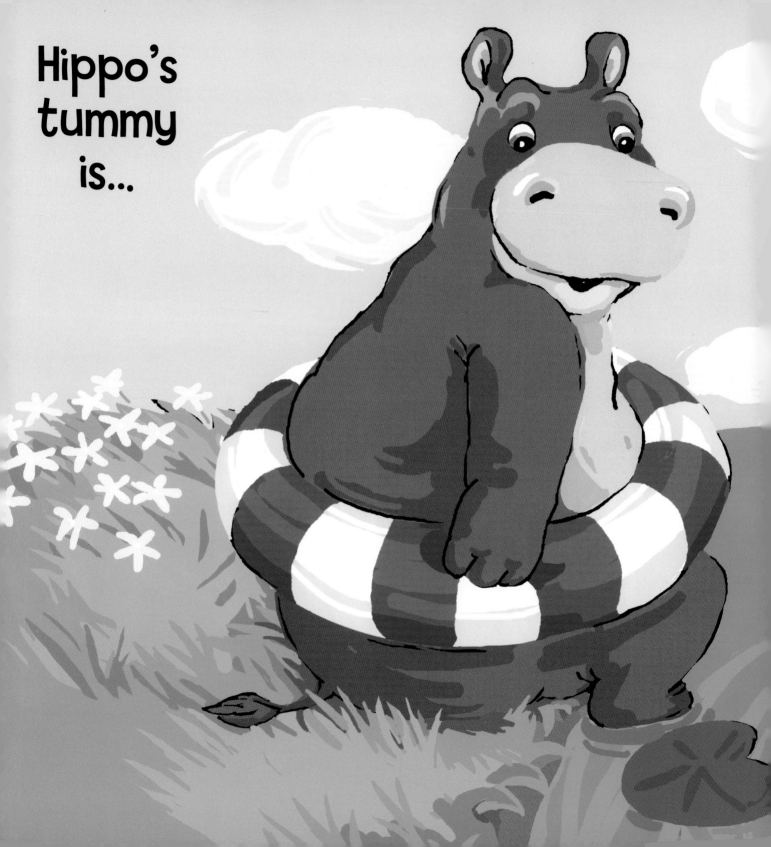

Hippo's
tummy
is...

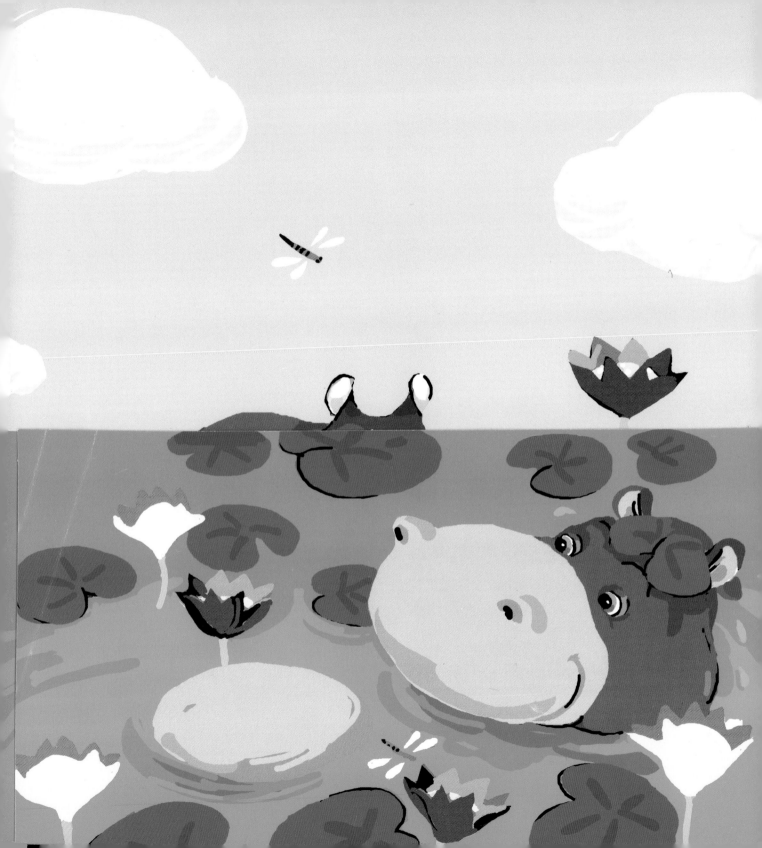

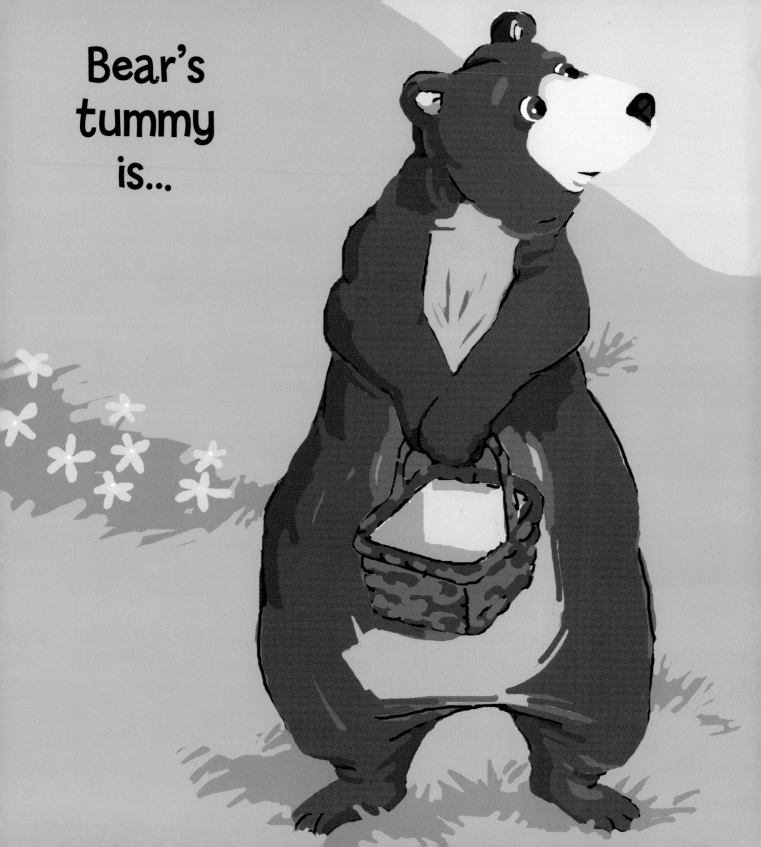

Bear's
tummy
is...

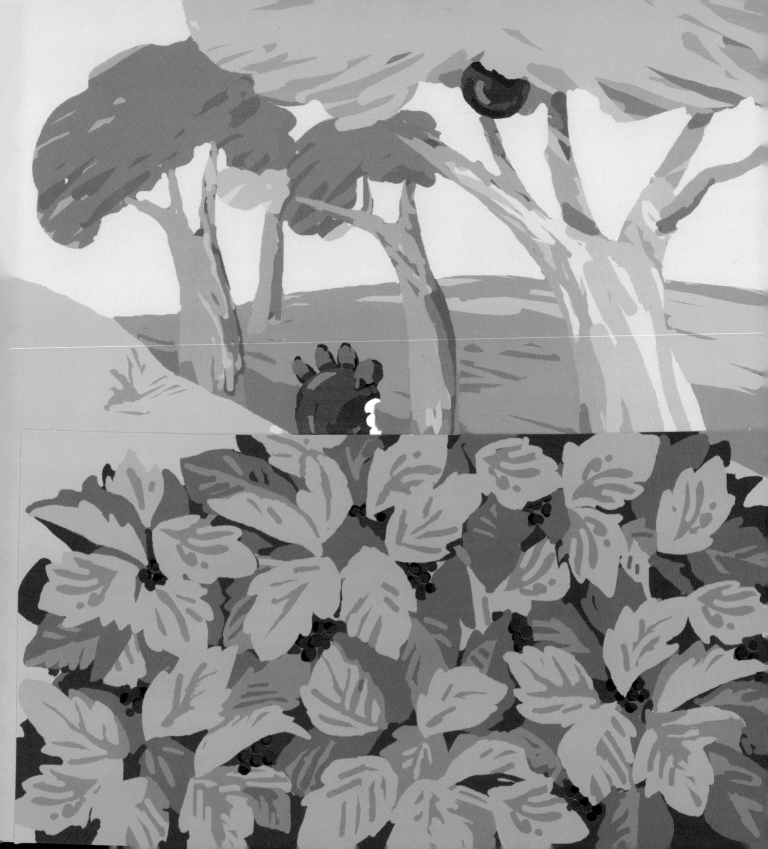

Gorilla's tummy...

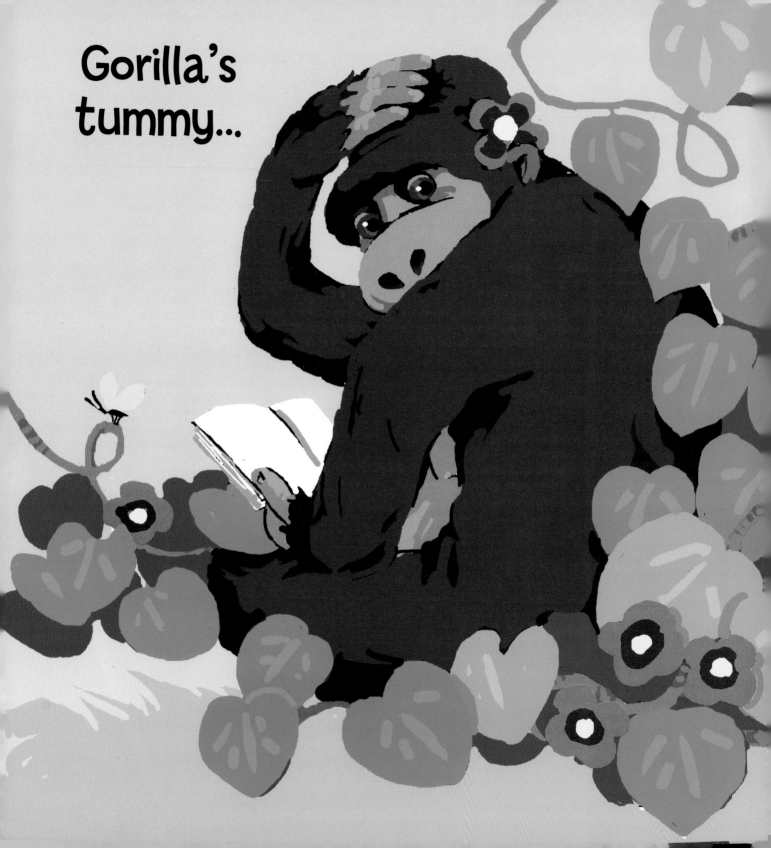

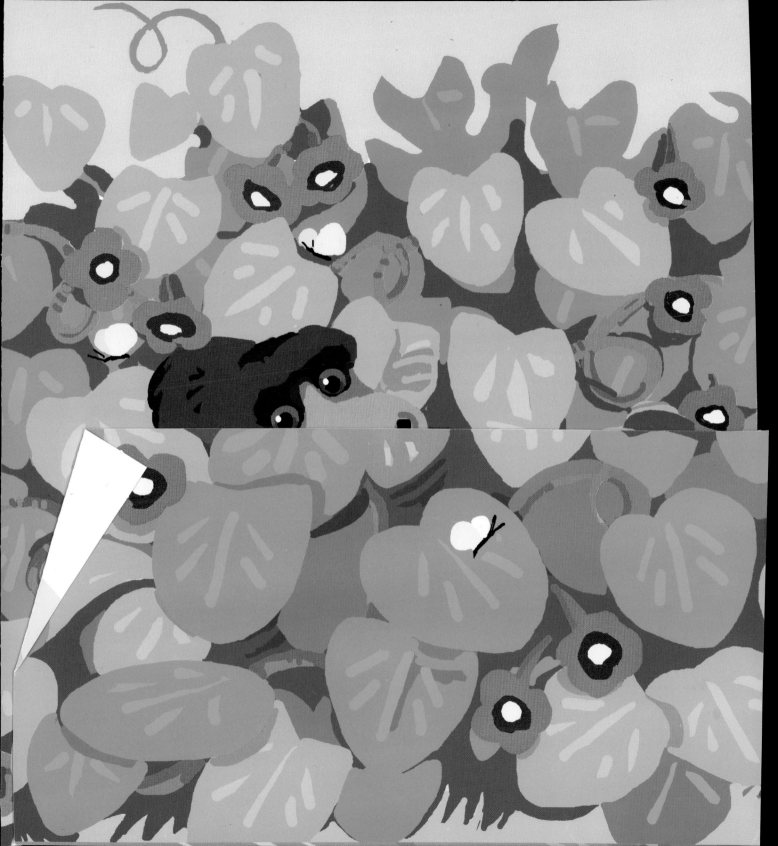

And
when
you're
tired
and
need a
rest...